PERCY

Based on *The Railway Series* by the Rev. W. Awdry

Illustrations by
Robin Davies and Creative Design

EGMONT

First published in Great Britain 2004
by Egmont Books Limited
239 Kensington High Street, London W8 6SA
All Rights Reserved

Thomas the Tank Engine & Friends

A BRITT ALLCROFT COMPANY PRODUCTION

Based on The Railway Series by The Rev W Awdry

© Gullane (Thomas) LLC 2004

ISBN 1 4052 1035 4
9 10
Printed in Great Britain

*T*his is a story about Percy the little green tank engine. He was very cheeky and loved playing tricks on the other engines. But one day he needed to be brave …

Percy loved playing tricks on the other engines. But these tricks sometimes got him into trouble.

One morning he was being very cheeky indeed. "Peep, peep! Hurry up!" he whistled to Gordon. "Your express train's ready."

Gordon thought he was late and came puffing out. But when he looked around there was only a train of dirty coal trucks!

"Ha, ha!" laughed Percy. But Gordon didn't think it was funny at all.

Next it was James' turn. Percy told James to stay in the shed because The Fat Controller was coming to see him.

James was a very proud engine, and thought that The Fat Controller must want him to pull a Special train. He stayed in the shed all day, and nothing his Driver could do would make him move.

The other engines were very annoyed. They had to do James' work as well as their own.

At last, The Fat Controller arrived. He was very cross with James. But he was even more angry with Percy when James explained what had happened.

When Percy arrived back at the Yard, The Fat Controller was waiting for him.

"You shouldn't waste time playing silly tricks, Percy!" shouted The Fat Controller. "You should be a Useful Engine."

Later that week, Thomas brought the Sunday School children to the beach. He asked Percy if he could take them home for him.

Percy thought that it sounded like very hard work. But he promised Thomas he would help.

The children had a lovely day. But by the afternoon, there were dark clouds overhead. Suddenly there was thunder and lightning, and the rain came lashing down! The children hurried to the station.

Annie and Clarabel were waiting for them at the platform. The children scrambled into the warm carriages.

"Percy, take the children home quickly, please," ordered the Stationmaster.

The rain poured down on Percy's boiler. "Ugh!" he shivered. He thought about pretending that he had broken down, so another engine would have to go instead of him. But then he remembered his promise. He must make sure the children got home safely.

Percy set off, bravely. But his Driver was worried. The rain was very heavy now and the river was rising fast.

The rain was getting in Percy's eyes and he couldn't see where he was going.

Suddenly he found himself in deep water. "Oooh, my wheels!" shivered Percy. But he struggled on.

"Oooshsh!" he hissed. The rain was beginning to put his fire out!

Percy's Driver decided to stop the train in a cutting. The Guard went to find a telephone. He returned looking very worried.

"We couldn't go back if we wanted to," he said. "The bridge near the junction is down."

They would have to carry on to the next station. But Percy's fire had nearly gone out, and they needed more wood to keep it going. "We'll have to pull up the floorboards and burn them!" said the Fireman.

Soon they had plenty of wood. Percy's fire burned well and he felt warm and comfortable again.

Suddenly, there came a "Buzz! Buzz! Buzz!" Harold was flying overhead.

"Oh dear!" thought Percy, sadly. "Harold has come to laugh at me."

Bump! Something thudded on Percy's boiler. A parachute had landed on top of him! Harold hadn't come to laugh. He was dropping hot drinks for everyone!

Everyone had a hot cocoa and felt much better.

Percy had got some steam up now. "Peep! Peep! Thank you, Harold!" he whistled. "Come on, let's go!"

As Percy started to move, the water began to creep up and up and up. It began to put his fire out again!

"Oooshsh!" shivered Percy.

Percy was losing steam, but he bravely carried on. "I promised Thomas," he panted. "I must keep my promise!"

The Fireman piled his fire high with wood. "I must do it," Percy gasped. "I must, I must, I must!"

Percy made a last great effort, and cleared the flood!

"Three cheers for Percy!" called the Vicar, and the children cheered as loudly as they could!

Harold arrived with The Fat Controller.

"Harold told me you were splendid, Percy." said The Fat Controller. "He says he can beat you at some things, but not at being a submarine! I don't know what you've both been doing, but I do know that you're a Really Useful Engine."

"Oh, thank you, Sir!" whispered Percy, happily.

The news of Percy's adventure soon got back to the Station. Gordon and James heard all about how Percy had kept his promise and travelled through the terrible storm to bring the children home safely. They both thought he was very brave and forgave him for all his tricks.

Percy realised that although playing tricks could be fun, it was much more important to be a Really Useful Engine!

The Thomas Story Library is THE definitive collection of stories about Thomas and ALL his Friends.

You can buy the Collector's Pack containing the first ten books for £24.99!

ISBN 1 4052 0827 9

5 more Thomas Story Library titles will be chuffing into your local bookshop in September 2005:

Trevor
Bertie
Diesel
Daisy
Spencer

And there are even more
Thomas Story Library books to follow later!

So go on, start your Thomas Story Library NOW!

A Fantastic Offer for Thomas the Tank Engine Fans!

In every Thomas Story Library book like this one, you will find a special token. Collect 6 Thomas tokens and we will send you a brilliant Thomas poster, and a double-sided bedroom door hanger!
Simply tape a £1 coin in the space above, and fill out the form overleaf.

TO BE COMPLETED BY AN ADULT

To apply for this great offer, ask an adult to complete the coupon below
and send it with a pound coin and 6 tokens, to:
THOMAS OFFERS, PO BOX 715, HORSHAM RH12 5WG

☐ Please send a Thomas poster and door hanger. I enclose 6 tokens
plus a £1 coin. (Price includes P&P)

Fan's name...

Address...

....Postcode.............................

Date of birth...

Name of parent/guardian..

Signature of parent/guardian...

Please allow 28 days for delivery. Offer is only available while stocks last. We reserve the right to change
the terms of this offer at any time and we offer a 14 day money back guarantee. This does not affect your
statutory rights.

☐ Data Protection Act: If you do not wish to receive other similar offers from us or companies we
recommend, please tick this box. Offers apply to UK only.